Disney Junior

MICKEY MOUSE ROADSTER RACERS

Coloring & Activity Book

By Steve Behling

bendon®

The BENDON name, logo and
Tear and Share are trademarks of
Bendon, Ashland, OH 44805.

Here's Mickey in his Daily Driver.

But it can transform into a supercool roadster!

His pals have roadsters, too!

Mickey and Donald like to race.

They help each other get ready.

Can you find and circle the only tire that will fit Donald's roadster?

Look at Donald go!

Connect the dots to see what Donald's drawing now.

"Welcome to the Race for the Rigatoni Ribbon!"

"Rigatoni Racers . . . rev up! Get set! Go!"

**Piston Pietro thinks he can beat
Donald and the roadster racers.**

It's the old "Pizza Pie Flip-and-Fly." Piston Pietro is cheating!

© Disney

"I've got your back, Minnie!"

Find and cross out all the pizzas.

Answer:

Goofy loves pizza!

Help Goofy and Piston Pietro find their way to the finish line.

Start

Finish

Answer:

"ROCKIN' AND RACIN'!"

"WINNING IN STYLE!"

When Minnie and Daisy aren't racing, they run a small business called the Happy Helpers!

The Happy Helpers will take care of your cat . . .

. . . teach you how to hula dance . . .

The Happy Helpers help out all around the world, including cleaning Big Ben in London!

Which gear completes each sequence?

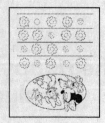

The Happy Helpers help out all around the world, including cleaning Big Ben in London!

Which gear completes each sequence?

Clara Cluck needs the Happy Helpers to egg-sit.

The Happy Helpers are on their way!

Pluto and Daisy check out Clara's egg.

Color and cut out the bows to decorate Clara's egg!

Clara's egg is hatching!

"We have to find Clara before her egg hatches!"

The Hot Diggity Hot Dog food trailer is out of control!

Minnie and Daisy help Clara welcome twins.

Can you spot six hot-diggity differences in the second picture?

"CRUISIN' THROUGH!"

"LIFE IN THE FASHION LANE!"

Pete is pals with Mickey.

Pete does not like to lose!

**Sometimes Pete breaks the rules
because he wants so badly to win.**

Help Pete follow the trail of hot dogs up, down, left, and right to find Goofy. Don't step on any oil slicks!

Start

Finish

Answer:

Pete is not always nice, but sometimes he does the right thing!

Pete learns to race for fun, not just to win.

Which piece completes this Pete puzzle?

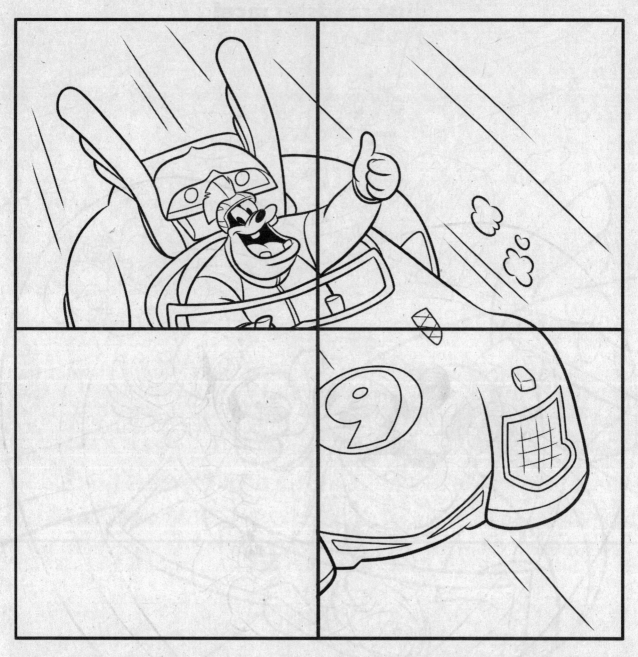

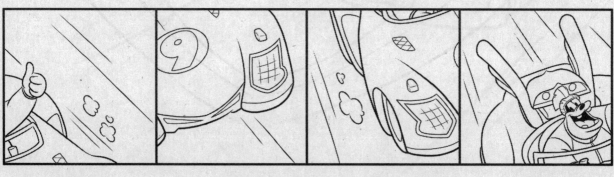

A.   B.   C.   D.

It's the anniversary of Mickey and Minnie's first roadster race!

Meanwhile, sneaky Sir Lord Pete takes the Queen's Royal Ruby.

Circle the missing Royal Ruby to help the police officer!

Answer:

Sir Lord Pete tosses the Royal Ruby before he can be caught!

"A raceversary gift? For me?"

"The ruby will be safe with Sir Lord Pete!"

Daisy catches the Royal Ruby!

© Disney

Find the path that leads to Goofy and keeps the Royal Ruby away from Sir Lord Pete!

Answer: D

"ROADSTER READY"

"You're all washed up, Sir Lord Pete!"

Put the picture in order to tell the story!

A

B

C

D

The birthday party is almost over.
Where is the cake?

The Happy Helpers are baking a birthday cake for someone special!

Find and circle the things the Happy Helpers need to bake a new cake.

flour

Sugar

PLUTO

Answers:

"We're on our way with the cake!"

Minnie and Daisy baked a brand-new cake!

"Help! These crazy skates have no brakes!"

See if you can find the silly differences in the picture below.

The Roadster Racers drive all around the world.

© Disney

They love to race!

Think Donald is driving an ordinary car?
Donald's Daily Driver can become...

...his Cabin Cruiser. *Splash!*

Pick a roadster, and find your way to the trophy!

Minnie calls her roadster Pink Thunder.

Daisy drives the stylish Snapdragon.

Goofy can drive *and* shower in the Turbo Tubster!

© Disney

"I've heard there's so much to do in Madrid!"

Mickey and the Roadster Racers arrive in Spain.

Help Mickey and Minnie find the only door without a bull.

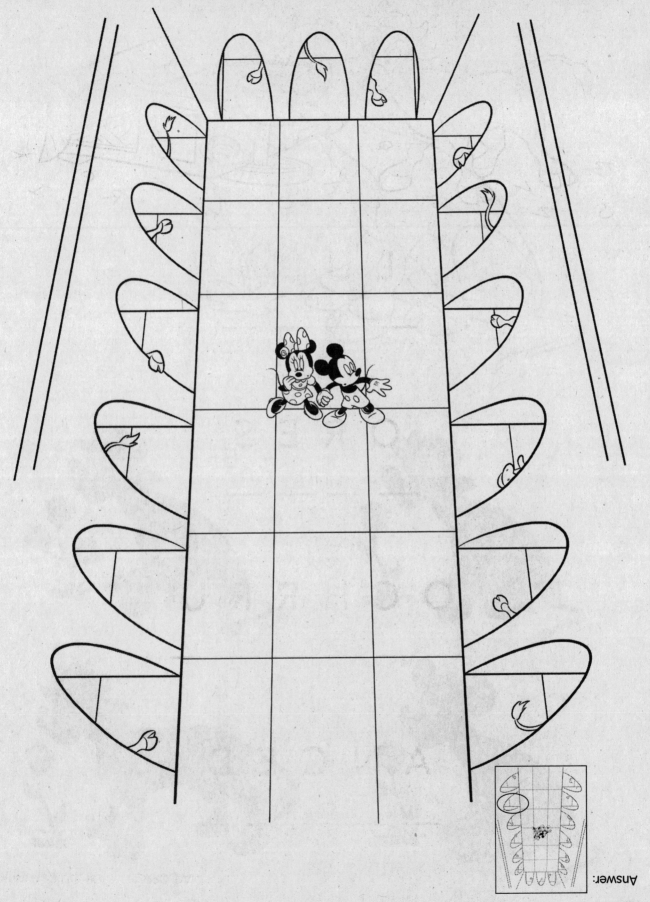

Answer:

Which shadow is an exact match for Francisco the bull?

A.

B.

C.

D.

It's your turn! Check out Goofy's silly moves, then create your own daffy dance!

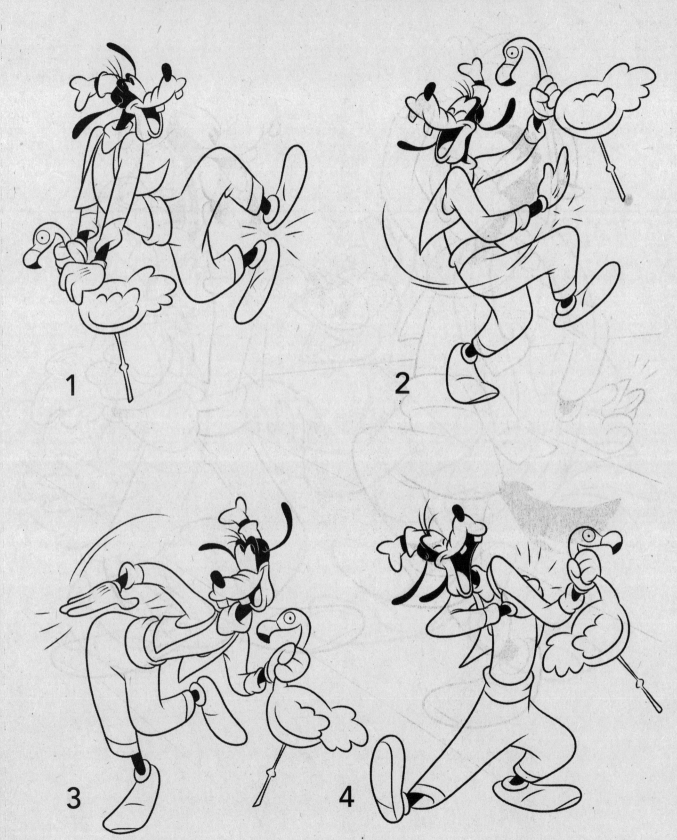

"I am Panchito Romero Miguel Junipero Francisco Quintero González III. But you may call me Panchito."

Donald ate something super spicy!
What will cool him down?

Answer:

Donald can't sing. Daisy has to take his place!

"This was a perfecto day!"

"Team Mickey on the go!"